Ghostville Elementary®

A Very Haunted Holiday

D0026958

Find out more spooky secrets about

Ghostville Elementary®

Ghostville Elementary®

A Very Haunted Holiday

by Marcia Thornton Jones
and
Debbie Dadey

illustrated by Guy Francis

A
LITTLE APPLE
PAPERBACK

SCHOLASTIC INC.

New York   Toronto   London   Auckland   Sydney
Mexico City   New Delhi   Hong Kong   Buenos Aires

ISBN-13: 978-0-439-88361-0
ISBN-10: 0-439-88361-X

12 11 10 9 8 7 6 5 4 3   8 9 10 11/0

Printed in the U.S.A.   40
First printing, December 2006

To Allison and Will:
May every day be worth celebrating.
—MTJ

To Jessica Day and the Day family
—DD

Contents

THE LEGEND
Sleepy Hollow Elementary School's
Online Newspaper

This Just In:

The halls have been decked! Sleepy Hollow Elementary is getting ready for the holidays. Rumor has it that the third graders in the basement are really in the spirit of the season. In fact, maybe they have a little too much spirit! Decorations are flying and strange gifts are being planned.

Could it have something to do with the fact that the basement is haunted? If those ghosts get out of control, Ghostville Elementary won't have a *happy* holiday — it will have a *haunted* holiday!

Stay tuned to find out more!

Yours truly,
Justin Thyme

1
Mismatched Ghost

"Deck the halls with boughs of holly!" Cassidy sang at the top of her lungs.

Cassidy and her two friends, Jeff and Nina, stood in the basement hallway outside their third-grade classroom. It was almost time for the morning bell to ring.

"Shh," Jeff warned. "The ghosts will hear you."

There were rumors that the basement of Sleepy Hollow Elementary was haunted by ghosts. Jeff, Nina, and Cassidy didn't believe in rumors. They believed in facts. The truth was, they had seen the ghosts with their very own eyes, more than once. In fact, they saw the ghosts almost every day!

"I can't help it!" Cassidy said. "I LOVE Christmas! Fa-la-la-la-la, la-la-la-la!" She

1

held out her arms and twirled in a circle. Round and round she went. Her blond hair twirled with her.

"Watch out!" Nina shrieked. But she was too late.

The air in the hall-way glowed with green glitter. The sparkles got thicker until the outline of a boy appeared. A *ghost* boy. Nina and Jeff knew who it was. Ozzy.

Cassidy was too busy spinning to see it. She twirled right through the ghost.

"AHHHHH!" Cassidy yelped. The green glitter cloud scattered like a glass Christmas ornament shattering into pieces. Cassidy fell down. Hard. Goose bumps raced up her arms and her teeth chattered. It felt like she had just been swimming in a pool full of snowballs.

"Watch where you're going!" Ozzy

cried when he pulled himself back together.

Nina opened her mouth to speak, but no words came out. The classroom ghosts always gave her the creeps, but today was even worse than usual. Ozzy's head was on backward and one of his arms stuck out of his belly button.

For once, Jeff was speechless, too.

Cassidy stood up and faced Ozzy. "I think you're ... um ... a little mismatched," she said as politely as she could.

"Mismatched?" Ozzy asked. "What do you mean?"

"You ... er ... aren't put together exactly the right way," Nina said, pointing.

Cassidy giggled.

Jeff nudged her with his sneaker. "Shh," he warned. "Don't make him mad."

Ozzy glanced down at his mixed-up

body. "Oops, sorry," he said. "I was too excited to notice." The ghost somersaulted through the air like a towel tumbling in a dryer. When he stopped, his head and his arm were back in the correct places and facing the right way.

"Better?" he asked the three kids, like it was normal to rearrange body parts.

Cassidy nodded.

"So, it's that time of year, isn't it?" Ozzy asked.

"What time?" Nina asked.

"Christmas!" Ozzy said, turning to Cassidy. "I heard you singing!"

Cassidy blushed. "It's my favorite time of the year," she admitted. "I couldn't help myself."

"It's a ghost's favorite time, too," Ozzy said with a grin. "Because it's the most MAGICAL time! We ghosts really get into the 'spirit' of the holidays. Wait until the others find out!" Then he popped out of sight, just as the morning bell rang.

5

2
Holiday Horror

"Most magical?" Cassidy asked her friends as they walked into the classroom. "What did he mean by that?"

Jeff pulled off his hat. "I have no idea," he said. "But since it was Ozzy who said it, it can't be good."

The three friends tried to forget about the ghosts as they hung up their coats and backpacks. By that time, the rest of the third graders had made their way into the classroom.

"Take your seats quickly!" Mr. Morton told the class. "I have wonderful news!"

Just then, Jeff noticed several green clouds forming right over Mr. Morton's head.

Pop!

Pop!
Pop!

Ozzy, his little sister Becky, and their ghost dog, Huxley, took shape in midair. Becky floated down and perched on Mr. Morton's desk. Huxley sniffed the teacher's shoe. Ozzy hovered over Mr. Morton's head.

Mr. Morton had no idea that anyone but his students were listening to every word he said. Ghosts were like that. They could decide who got to see and hear

them. So far, the ghosts had only appeared to Jeff, Cassidy, and Nina.

"I had a wonderful idea last night," Mr. Morton announced.

A couple of kids rolled their eyes. A boy named Andrew groaned out loud. Mr. Morton was known for coming up with ideas. Usually they involved lots and lots of work.

"Hanukah! Christmas! Kwanzaa!" Mr. Morton continued. "The holidays are coming, and I think we should make this a season of giving in our classroom, too."

Andrew sat up in his chair. "That's a great idea! What are you going to give *me*?"

Mr. Morton wiped chalk dust from his glasses and looked right at Andrew. "I don't want you to think about what you want to *get*," Mr. Morton said. "This year, I want you to concentrate on what you can *give*."

Mr. Morton pointed to the bulletin

board. Two huge blank pieces of paper were stapled up to it. "This year, instead of making a long list of things you want, I want us to brainstorm together and make a single list of good gift ideas for others."

Andrew slumped down in his chair as Mr. Morton continued telling the class about his plan. "Then everyone can use the ideas and bring in a gift for our class-room celebration. Nobody will be left out — and I mean *nobody!* Isn't that wonderful?"

As soon as the ghosts heard Mr. Morton's announcement, they went into hyper-drive. Becky shot up into the air. Ozzy turned cartwheels. Huxley danced on his back legs.

"Presents!" Becky cheered. Of course, only Jeff, Cassidy, and Nina could hear her. "We're all getting presents!"

That's when Jeff noticed something truly frightening. He knew that ghosts had to concentrate extra-hard to touch

something in the real world. Becky was usually the worst at concentrating, so she tended to go straight through things. But that wasn't what happened as the ghosts celebrated. Without even pausing, Becky pushed aside a stack of papers. They tumbled to the floor.

"Oh, no!" Jeff whispered to Nina and Cassidy. "This can only mean one thing. A holiday horror!"

3
Squuuueeaaakk!

"Stop singing," Jeff told Cassidy during spelling.

"I'm not singing," Cassidy said.

"Be quiet," Nina whispered to Cassidy when they worked on math problems. "Your humming is driving me crazy."

Cassidy shook her head. "I am NOT humming."

Nina frowned. She wanted to catch Cassidy in the act, but when Nina watched, she saw that her friend was quiet. If it wasn't Cassidy humming, then who was it?

Nina looked around the room. Andrew was flicking little pieces of eraser into Barbara's hair. The twins, Carla and Darla, had their heads bent over their papers. The rest of the class was hard at work, too. Nobody was singing. Nobody else seemed to hear anything. Still, Nina heard music.

It wasn't peaceful music, either. Nina finally put her hands over her ears to drown out the loud squeals of "We wish you a merry Christmas!"

Jeff nudged her in the ribs. "Look," he said, pointing.

Above the bookshelf, a ghost choir sang. Loudly. The ghost named Calliope tucked her violin under her chin and played.

SQUUUUEEAAAKK!
SCRATCHHHHHHH!
SQUEEEEEEALLLL!

"We have to make them quiet down," Nina whispered. "I can't get any work done."

Jeff nodded. "We'll get Fs on our report cards if we have to listen to that all through the holidays."

"But how can we stop them?" Nina asked. Ghosts did not listen to people.

They did exactly what they wanted, when they wanted.

"I have an idea," Jeff said. He jumped out of his seat and walked up to Mr. Morton's chart. Under gift ideas, Jeff wrote in big letters: **PEACE AND QUIET.** Then he looked right at the ghosts.

The singing stopped. The violin stopped. Nina took a deep breath. Jeff's idea had worked, but the quiet only lasted a minute.

"Yeee-hawww!" Ozzy screamed. He blasted toward Jeff like a rocket.

4
Disgusting

Jeff ducked out of the way just in time. Ozzy screeched to a stop next to the chart, grabbed Jeff's pencil, and scribbled. Jeff looked around the room to make sure no one else had noticed him ducking or the pencil moving by itself. Thankfully, only Nina and Cassidy were watching. Finally, Jeff snatched the pencil back and hurried to his seat.

The ghosts disappeared with a *pop*, but then another noise caught Nina's attention. She heard a jingling, or maybe it was a jangling. Suddenly, Olivia stood at the classroom door. A big set of keys dangled from her bright red overalls. No one knew exactly how old Olivia was, but she'd been the janitor at Spooky Hollow Elementary for longer than anyone could remember. A small white mouse jumped out of her pocket, scurried across the room, and hid behind the bookcase.

"A mouse!" Nina squealed.

Mr. Morton jumped up from his chair in surprise.

Carla and Darla pulled their legs onto their chairs and started crying. Andrew raced out of his seat toward the bookcase. "I'll stomp on it!"

Olivia grabbed Andrew by the collar.

"No one is going to hurt Gaylor. He's just a bit shy."

Cassidy shivered. "He's disgusting."

Olivia shook her head and her long earrings tinkled. "Every creature is different. He probably thinks *you're* disgusting."

Andrew laughed. "I think Cassidy's disgusting, too."

"She is no such thing," Olivia said, scowling. "Being different is good.

Differences add spice to life. It makes every day worth celebrating. You should all keep that in mind. Especially at this time of year."

Mr. Morton frowned at Andrew while Olivia bent down and held out her hand. The mouse scooted from behind the bookshelf right into Olivia's open palm.

Olivia dropped Gaylor into her pocket. "Sorry to disturb you. I just wanted to let you know that it's snowing. Outside recess has been cancelled for today."

The whole class groaned, but Mr. Morton nodded and said, "Thank you, Olivia." Olivia disappeared down the hallway.

"All right," Mr. Morton said. "Let's finish our math."

Andrew groaned again and sat back down in his seat. He hadn't finished his math yet, but that didn't keep him from looking around the room. When he saw the gift chart, he shouted, "Look at that!"

5
Mystery Gifts

"What are we going to do?" Nina asked her two best friends the next morning. Nina, Cassidy, and Jeff always walked to school together.

"I'll tell you what we're going to do," Jeff said. "Nothing. That's all we can do."

When the rest of the third graders had seen Ozzy's writing on Mr. Morton's gift chart, Jeff had taken the blame.

"Nobody is going to believe that you really think knickerbockers and a frock coat are good holiday gifts," Nina said. "And what are we going to do when the other ghosts start adding to the list?"

"I'll think of something," Jeff said as

they turned up the sidewalk toward Sleepy Hollow Elementary School.

"We have to stop the ghosts before they ruin the holidays for everyone!" Nina jumped over a crack. "What do you think, Cassidy?"

"Huh?" Cassidy asked. "Were you talking to me?"

"Of course we were. What's wrong with you?"

"Sorry," Cassidy said. "I was thinking about my grandfather."

"What about him?" Jeff asked as they reached the front door of the school.

Cassidy sighed. "He's usually nice. Nosy, but nice. But lately he's been a real grouch. He doesn't even want to play checkers. Last night he turned off the Christmas special I was watching on TV."

Nina patted Cassidy on the shoulder. "I know exactly what you mean. My *abuela* is acting the same way. Maybe grandparents don't enjoy the holidays."

Cassidy sighed. She didn't like it when her grandfather was grumpy. But thoughts of her grandfather disappeared as soon as she entered the classroom. A big crowd of kids had clustered around the bulletin board.

"Look!" Allison said.

Carla pointed to Mr. Morton's chart. "Who wrote . . ."

". . . that?" Darla finished.

Cassidy, Nina, and Jeff pushed their

way through the crowd. Somebody had added to the chart again. The handwriting was squiggly and the words were misspelled, but that's not what worried Jeff. He was worried because he knew these things weren't written by any of the third graders. They were written by the ghosts.

fig pUdding
Ribbens and boUghs
Kwill and Inkwell
Bolt of Gingham
fiddel and bow

"Ribbons and bows, ribbons and bows," Andrew joked. "Jeff's going to wear ribbons and bows!"

The tips of Jeff's ears turned red. The last thing he wanted was ribbons and bows, but he couldn't say a word. If he did, it might give away the ghosts. So he took the blame . . . again.

Right before lunch, Mr. Morton set up

an art center where the kids could make holiday decorations. "We'll decorate the room," Mr. Morton explained. "Feel free to use the center during your free time."

What Mr. Morton didn't know was that the ghosts in his classroom had plenty of free time. Once the class returned from lunch, red and green streamers criss-crossed the room.

"Look what Jeff did," Andrew shouted. "He used up ALL the decorations. That's not fair."

The kids looked at Jeff. So did Mr. Morton. Jeff did the only thing he could think of. "I'm sorry," he said. "I got carried away."

Mr. Morton wiped a spot on his glasses and looked at all the decorations. "When did you do this?" he asked. It was a good thing Jeff was a quick thinker. "While you were eating lunch I asked to be excused. Then I came down here and, well, decorated."

"We wondered where you went," Nina hurried to add.

Mr. Morton sighed. "I wish you were this fast at getting homework done!"

While the rest of the kids marched into the room, Cassidy patted Jeff on the back. "How did the ghosts get so much done so fast?" she asked Jeff and Nina quietly.

"Magic," Jeff told the girls. "Holiday magic. I've been watching them. Remember when Ozzy said that ghosts like this time of year? Well, I think holiday magic makes ghosts even more powerful. They can do things in the real world easier than usual."

"Great," Cassidy sighed. "Just what we need."

The ghostly decorations were a little old-fashioned. But that wasn't half as bad as what happened the next day.

6
Jingle All the Way!

"What's that smell?" Nina asked as she and her friends made their way down the hall to their classroom.

"If my grandpa was still talking to us, he would say it's the smell of an old-fashioned Christmas," Cassidy said with a sigh.

"Is he still being grumpy?" Jeff asked Cassidy.

Cassidy sighed again. "He's even *worse*. Last night, when my mom brought home our brand-new tree and took it out of the box, he stomped out of the room. He said something about Christmas not being like it used to be. Now he won't even talk to us."

"What does he expect?" Nina asked. "Lots of people use artificial trees."

"I guess he thinks we should hike out to a forest and cut down our own tree," Cassidy said, "like in the 'good old days.' But that'll never happen because my family is too busy."

Nina nodded. "My *abuela* keeps talking about how she used to celebrate the holidays in Mexico. I tried to tell her that things are done differently here, but that just made her mad."

Jeff opened the door to the classroom. As soon as the kids stepped inside, they

froze. They couldn't believe what they saw. A huge pine tree took up one whole corner of the room. It was decorated from top to bottom with pine cones, popcorn, and berries. There was even a paper angel at the top.

"Oh, my," Mr. Morton was saying. "My, my, my." He wiped chalk dust from his glasses and peered at the giant tree. "Trees are not allowed in classrooms," he muttered. "Not allowed. Not allowed."

"Why not?" Andrew asked. "It's Christmas!"

"Allergies," Mr. Morton explained. "And some people don't celebrate their holidays with trees. What will the principal do when she finds out? She'll be mad. Mad, mad, mad!"

Mr. Morton stood before the tree and wrung his hands. Nina, Cassidy, and Jeff didn't want Mr. Morton to get in trouble. Sure, their teacher made them work, and he sometimes came up with silly ideas. Still, the three kids liked their teacher, and they knew he tried hard.

Just then, a cloud of green mist surrounded the tree. Slowly, shape after shape appeared until all the ghosts appeared as eerie decorations perched on the tree branches.

Becky danced along one of the branches. Calliope sat on the tippy-top of the tree and played her violin. Ozzy dangled from a branch and swatted at Andrew's cap.

"Jingle bells, jingle bells," Ozzy sang.

"JINGLE ALL THE WAY!" the rest of the ghosts chimed in. They sang so loudly, they broke the human-ghost sound barrier!

"What was that?" Mr. Morton gasped.

"I bet Jeff knows!" Andrew yelled. "It's probably some of his movie magic!" Jeff planned to be a famous director. He often bragged about how to make movies.

Mr. Morton looked at Jeff. "Is that true?" he asked. "Did *you* do that?"

7
Surprises

The whole class was watching him, so Jeff did the only thing he could do. He fibbed. "I don't know where this came from." It wasn't a total lie. After all, he didn't know where the ghosts had gotten all the decorations, or how they'd brought the tree inside.

It seemed like Mr. Morton didn't believe Jeff. Cassidy had to do something to help her best friend. "I bet someone is trying to surprise us," she said. "Maybe it was Olivia."

Mr. Morton thought hard. "Maybe she did."

Carla giggled. "This is a much nicer surprise than a . . . ."

". . . math test," Darla finished for her twin.

Mr. Morton smiled. "I suppose you're right about that."

"Look!" Andrew said. "Somebody left another surprise on your desk, Mr. Morton!"

"Oh no," Nina muttered. She didn't want any more surprises. She hoped this one wasn't from the ghosts.

It was.

Mr. Morton held up a long skinny package, wrapped in drawing paper. "Who gave me this?"

Cassidy looked around the room. None of the kids held up their hands, but one ghost waved his hand in the air. Nate flew over to Mr. Morton and grinned. "That's from me," Nate said proudly. Cassidy, Nina, and Jeff were the only ones who could hear him.

Mr. Morton unwrapped the gift. "Um, very nice," he said. "Though I'm not exactly sure what it is." He held up a stick. One end had been sharpened into a point.

"It's a pointing stick," Nate said, grinning widely. "I whittled it myself."

"A stick?" Andrew muttered. He was totally unaware that Nate was hovering near Mr. Morton. "Somebody gave you a dumb stick?"

"Andrew," Mr. Morton said. "That tone is not necessary. This is a very nice stick."

Andrew shrugged and muttered under his breath. "No, it's not. It's a dumb gift, just like the rest of those gift ideas on the list."

Nate floated beside Mr. Morton's desk, looking sad. Nina felt so sorry for Nate. He'd worked hard to make a nice present, and Mr. Morton didn't even know what it was.

Nina raised her hand. "I think that's a pointing stick," she said. "Teachers used those a long time ago."

"I bet you're right." Mr. Morton said. "Did you make this, Nina?"

Nina shook her head while Andrew muttered. "Stupid, stupid, stupid."

Andrew must have said "stupid" one too many times, because Nate flew through the air and pounced on him. Andrew rolled on the ground, knocking

over a trash can. Papers scattered everywhere.

"Andrew!" Mr. Morton shouted. "Will
you quit goofing off?"

Andrew sat up and slapped at the goose
bumps on his arms. "Who pushed me?"
he asked. The rest of the kids just giggled. Someone had knocked him down,

but no one was near him. At least, no one that Andrew could see.

Nate floated around the classroom with a satisfied grin on his face. He looked like he'd just won a national wrestling championship. Unfortunately, Nate was not quite finished with Andrew.

8
I didn't do it!

Nate tripped Andrew when he got up to sharpen his pencil. Nate stood by Andrew's desk and knocked the papers off during social studies. Then Nate slammed Andrew's spelling book to the floor.

"Andrew," Mr. Morton said sternly. "Please control yourself."

"But I didn't do it!" Andrew sputtered.

"This is no time for stories, Andrew. Now, get to work," Mr. Morton said. The class bowed their heads over their spelling papers.

Mr. Morton frowned and wiped his glasses with a tissue. That gave Nate an idea. When Mr. Morton's back was turned, Nate flew over to the tissue box.

He pulled out a handful of tissues and squished them into balls. Then he flew behind Andrew and tossed the tissue balls at Carla.

"Mr. Morton! Andrew is throwing paper at me!" Carla said, dodging tissues.

Andrew looked up. Wadded-up tissues covered Carla's desk, and one was stuck in her hair. "I didn't do it," Andrew said.

"Andrew!" Mr. Morton said. "One more problem and you'll have to miss recess for the rest of the week."

"But I didn't do it!" Andrew insisted.

Nate rolled around the classroom floor, holding his tummy and laughing huge belly laughs. "That'll teach him to call me stupid!" he cried.

"How is Nate doing all of that?" Nina whispered to her two friends.

Cassidy's forehead was wrinkled with worry. "Ghosts usually have to concentrate very hard to move something in the real world, but Nate is doing it without a second thought," she said.

"It's the magic," Jeff said quietly. "Holiday magic."

At that moment, Nate floated by Nina's desk. "Please stop bothering Andrew before something bad happens," she whispered.

Nate stopped laughing and winked at Nina. "I'm just getting started. Watch this."

Nina watched in horror as Nate zipped through the air. In one quick motion, he yanked all of Andrew's hair until it stuck straight up.

"Ouch!" Andrew snapped. "Someone pulled my hair!"

Andrew glared at Darla, who sat behind him. "I didn't do it," she said.

Andrew looked around. He couldn't see Nate in front of him.

Nate took a deep breath, then blew. He blew so hard that Andrew's hair flew straight behind him. Andrew even fell out of his desk. Then Nate spun himself into a tornado. It was so strong that Andrew was caught up in the ghost wind.

"Help!" Andrew cried helplessly.

Mr. Morton couldn't see the ghost or the tornado, but he *could* see Andrew spinning around and around in the middle of the classroom.

"That's it!" Mr. Morton told Andrew. "No recess for you."

Immediately, Nate stopped spinning. Andrew plopped to the ground.

As Nate disappeared, Nina crossed her fingers and hoped that the ghost boy had finished bothering Andrew . . . for good.

9
Snake

"Seeing Andrew get in trouble yesterday was fun," Cassidy said.

Nina shook her head. "Nate was mean."

"But the look on Andrew's face was great," Jeff said. "I wish I'd caught it on video! It would win an award!"

"I hope Nate is finished with his ghost tricks," Nina said. "I want a nice quiet day today."

Unfortunately, the kids could tell there was a problem as soon as they reached the door that led down to the basement.

"Listen," Cassidy said, stopping her friends. Loud moaning echoed up the damp steps. That was followed by the sound of someone hitting the ground. Hard.

"That sounded bad," Nina said. "Very bad."

"We should run for help," Cassidy said.

Jeff shook his head. "Somebody down there needs help fast. We don't have time!"

The three friends peered down the steps. Cassidy swallowed. Nina took a deep breath. "It's now or never," Jeff said.

Step by step, the three friends went down into the shadows. They breathed in the damp basement air. The door to their classroom

46

stood wide open. "Let's get this over with," Cassidy said.

Slowly, they made their way down the hallway. When they reached the door, Jeff peeked inside.

"Oh, no!" he gasped.

Cassidy and Nina's curiosity got the best of them. They *had* to look.

Mr. Morton lay in a heap on the floor. A brightly colored paper chain zigzagged across the room and twisted around his arms and legs. Mr. Morton had been caught in it like a bug in a spider web!

"Help me!" Mr. Morton pleaded. "I've fallen and I can't get up!"

Cassidy, Nina, and Jeff quickly untangled their teacher from the paper chain.

47

"When I find out who is responsible for this," Mr. Morton said, "they will be in big, big trouble!"

The three kids gulped.

"Coffee. I need coffee," Mr. Morton mumbled as he hurried out the door and up the steps to the teachers' lounge.

Nina, Cassidy, and Jeff picked the torn pieces of paper chain up off the floor. They knew exactly who had made the chains, because she had been moaning the entire time.

Sadie was the saddest ghost to haunt Sleepy Hollow Elementary School. She was usually a sick shade of green and cried a lot, but the holidays had made Sadie happy. In fact, she had been so happy that she had spent the whole night making paper chains to decorate the classroom. And, thanks to holiday magic, Sadie had worked fast. Very fast. Now Mr. Morton had ruined her decorations. What was worse, Mr. Morton was mad.

"NO! NOOOOOOO! NOOOOOOOOO!"

Sadie wailed. She hovered in the middle of the paper chains and cried giant tears. They rolled down her cheeks and plopped to the floor.

"Stop that!" cried Becky, who had been sitting cross-legged on the floor. Now she stood up and shook her finger at Sadie. "You're ruining the present I'm making!"

"Present?" Cassidy repeated. "Why are you making a present?'

"For the celebration, silly. Mr. Morton said everyone was included," Becky said, like that explained everything. "But this sourpuss has ruined my paper dolls. And I worked all night on them!"

On the floor was a mountain of wet paper dolls. Becky stomped. She kicked. She pounded the air with her fists. She went into an all-out spinning-kicking-throwing tantrum. Sadie's paper chain was caught in Becky's whirlwind. Paper dolls were flung into the air. The paper chain twisted and turned until it was

knotted into a long snake that lashed out in all directions.

Cassidy dived behind Mr. Morton's desk. Nina cowered behind the trash can. Jeff fell flat on the floor and covered his head. "Help!" he screamed.

10
Cele-BOO-HOO-HOO-tion

"We have to do something," Jeff told his friends at recess. His breath floated in the cold December air like a ghost.

The rest of the third graders were building a big snow fort together. But Jeff, Nina, and Cassidy sat perched on the top rung of the monkey bars. Playing in the snow was the last thing on their minds.

"Becky was not happy that Sadie's tears ruined the gift she was making," Nina said.

"Sadie wasn't so happy about her paper chain getting torn up, either," Cassidy pointed out.

"Face it," Jeff said. "All the ghosts are upset. This is not how Christmas is supposed to be."

"Between the ghosts and my grandfather, this holiday is going to be ruined," Cassidy said softly. "Tell me, just how *is* Christmas supposed to be?"

Nina put her hand around her friend's shoulder. "Christmas is about sharing."

"It's about family and friends," Jeff added.

"The holidays are all about putting aside your differences and getting along," Nina said.

"And they're about believing, too," Jeff finished.

"Even believing in ghosts?" Cassidy asked.

"Even in ghosts," Nina and Jeff said together, laughing.

"Well," Cassidy said slowly. "If the holidays include all that, then we have to get busy. Otherwise, our Christmas celebration will be a cele-BOO-tion!"

"What do you mean?" Nina asked.

"The ghosts are having trouble finishing their handmade gifts. They're already upset," Cassidy explained. "But what worries me most is how are we going to explain the extra ghostly gifts at the class party?"

Nina slapped her forehead. "I hadn't thought of that. The rest of the class will think WE brought those silly things."

"That's not the bad part," Jeff said softly.

"It can't get any worse," Nina said. "Can it?"

Jeff nodded. "Think about it. Mr. Morton has promised that no one will be left out. What will the ghosts do if there aren't any presents for them? There's nothing worse than feeling left out, especially during the holidays. And the ghosts have gone to so much trouble to make gifts for us!"

Nina plopped down on the ground. "If we don't do something fast, this holiday cele-BOO-tion will turn into a giant cele-BOO-HOO-HOO-tion!"

"But how can we explain those extra gifts and still keep the ghosts a secret?" Cassidy asked.

"I have a plan," Jeff said. "Listen . . ."

11
The Plan

Cassidy shook her head. "Nope. It won't work."

Jeff put his hands on his hips. "Do you have a better plan?"

Cassidy shrugged. "No."

"We have to do something," Nina said, agreeing with Jeff.

Jeff grinned and climbed down from the monkey bars. "Besides, my idea is in the spirit of Christmas. We're helping the ghosts."

"That's right. My parents give food to the homeless shelter all year long, but they give more during the holidays," Nina said, jumping to the ground. "This is the season for giving."

"That might be true," Cassidy said,

climbing down slowly. "But I still don't think Mr. Morton will let us do it."

Jeff grinned. "Mr. Morton doesn't have to know. We'll make it a surprise."

"A holiday surprise!" Nina cheered.

"Let's go to Principal Finkle and tell her what we want to do," Jeff said.

"Principal Finkle?" Cassidy squealed.

Nina shuddered. "No way! She gives me the creeps."

"We have to get her permission if we're

going to make this work," Jeff said, walking toward the school. "Hurry! Before recess is over."

Nina gulped. Cassidy frowned. Then they followed Jeff to the principal's office.

When they knocked on her office door, Ms. Finkle looked up from a pile of papers and gave them a mysterious smile. Her eyes studied them from behind dark-rimmed reading glasses. "What do you want?" she snapped as the kids came inside. Nina jumped and hid behind Cassidy.

None of the kids said a word until Cassidy nudged Jeff. "I . . . um, I mean, we want to surprise our teacher for the holidays," Jeff whispered.

Principal Finkle ran her long dagger-like fingernails through her dark hair. "Surprise? This sounds interesting."

"It is," Jeff agreed, "but it will take a lot of work."

Principal Finkle walked across her

office. Her high heels clicked on the tile floor. Nina gulped as the principal pulled her office door shut with a bang. They were trapped!

"Tell me exactly what you have in mind," Principal Finkle said, folding her arms across her chest.

12
Happy Holidays!

Andrew crammed a handful of cookies into his mouth. "Quit being so messy," Darla told him.

Carla nodded. "You're getting crumbs everywhere."

"Didn't they have crumbs in the olden days?" Andrew asked with his mouth full.

Nina laughed as Nate flew around the room picking up the crumbs. The ghosts were having a great time. Sadie and Becky were decorating sugar cookies behind the book-shelf. "This is so much fun!" Becky giggled.

Sadie wasn't her usual green. Instead, she sparkled a brilliant pink as she put yellow icing on a big star-shaped cookie.

All over the classroom, ghosts, kids, parents, and grandparents decorated cookies, opened presents, and ate old-fashioned treats. "This is the best popcorn ball I've ever tasted," Cassidy's grandfather said. "We used to make these all the time."

Cassidy smiled. "I'm glad you're having fun! You've been a little grumpy lately."

Her grandfather nodded. "I know I

have. I'm sorry, Cassidy. I guess I just missed how Christmas used to be."

"I know what you mean," Nina's *abuela* said. "Traditions are important."

Ms. Finkle walked up beside Nina and her grandmother. "That's why I thought this historical celebration would be nice. After all, we're celebrating the history of our old school."

"It's a wonderful surprise," Mr. Morton agreed. "Inviting everyone's families makes it even more special."

Jeff handed Cassidy's grandfather a present. "There are even gifts from long ago, too."

Cassidy's grandfather unwrapped a wooden yo-yo. His eyes sparkled. "Why, look at this! I haven't seen one of these in ages. This one looks hand-carved."

Nate danced a jig in the air around the yo-yo. "I made that," he sang. "I made that!"

"Whoever carved this is a very smart lad," Cassidy's grandfather exclaimed.

"And talented, too," Nina's *abuela* agreed. Nate glowed with pride.

Jeff's plan had gone off without a hitch. Once the rest of the kids found out their parents and grandparents were part of the celebration, they stopped arguing and worked together. They even had fun shopping for some of the old-fashioned gifts that the ghosts had put on the list. Nobody noticed that Nina, Jeff, and Cassidy brought a few extras to put under the tree. Nobody, that is, except for the ghosts. Everyone enjoyed opening their presents, and even the ghosts loved the stories the grandparents told of holidays long ago. They were all basking in the true 'spirit' of the holidays.

"Whew," Cassidy said to her friends. "It looks like we saved Christmas."

"I'm just tired of worrying about the ghosts' holiday magic," Nina said. "I'll be glad when the ghosts get back to normal."

Just then, the door swung open. Or

maybe it flew open. "Ho! Ho! Ho!" Olivia said. "Merry Christmas!"

Gaylor popped out of Olivia's big over-all pocket and hopped to the floor. Cocomo, the ghost cat, took one look at Gaylor's twitching whiskers and went into action. Huxley galloped after Cocomo. The mouse raced through the cookie dough with the two ghosts hot on his tail.

"AHHHHHHH!" screamed the kids.

"AHHHHHHH!" screamed the parents and grandparents.

"AHHHHHHH!" screamed Mr. Morton.

"I have a feeling," Jeff said as every-one scrambled away from the fleeing mouse, "that nothing will ever be normal at Ghostville Elementary!"

Authors' Note

How do you celebrate the winter holidays?

1.) Draw a picture of your family and friends celebrating.
2.) Write a paragraph about your celebration.
3.) Put your picture and paragraph together with the kids in your class to make a holiday book.
4.) Have a "Holiday Show and Tell" to share some of the things your family does to make the holidays special.

About the Authors

Marcia Thornton Jones and Debbie Dadey got into the *spirit* of writing when they worked together at the same school in Lexington, Kentucky. Since then, Debbie has *haunted* several states. She currently *haunts* Ft. Collins, Colorado, with her three children, three dogs, and husband. Marcia remains in Lexington, where she lives with her husband and two cats. Debbie and Marcia have fun with spooky stories. They have scared themselves silly with *The Adventures of the Bailey School Kids* and *The Bailey City Monsters* series. Debbie also writes the *Swamp Monster in Third Grade* series.